THIS BOOK BELONGS TO

....

For information address Disney Press, 1101 Flower Street,
Glendale, California 91201.

ISBN 978-1-4847-9955-0

FAC-038091-17174

Printed in the United States of America

Library of Congress Control Number: 2016948946

First Hardcover Edition, August 2017

1 3 5 7 9 10 8 6 4 2

For more Disney Press fun, visit www.disneybooks.com

We Are NOT Lost!

By **Marie Eden**
Illustrated by **Amy Mebberson**

Disney PRESS
LOS ANGELES • NEW YORK

MUNCH

MUNCH

PUMBAA!

What are you doing?
We're going to the
water hole.
Come on, **let's go!**

Boy, it's a SCORCHER!
OOH, I have an idea.
Let's go to the

WATER HOLE!

GEEZ.
Here we go again.

Pumbaa, where do you **think** we are going?

Come on, let's **GO!**

What is it, Pumbaa?

We are not lost. I know
EXACTLY where we are.

We have passed this tree
THREE times!

It is a
different tree.

It is the same tree.
Look, my snack is
still here.

That is a **DIFFERENT** snack.
Come on, let's **GO.**

Timon, STOP!

What is it **this time,** Pumbaa?

My snack is
getting away!

Pumbaa, you *just* ate!

Come on, let's go!

But, Timon, you always say you gotta put the past behind you. That snack was in the past.

And look, I found your FAVORITE!

Ooh, the cream-filled kind!

Well, maybe just one . . .

You want one?
They're **DELICIOUS!**

NO?
Your loss.

MMMM.
Slimy, but **satisfying.**

BOY,
those made me
THIRSTY.

OH! I KNOW!
Let's go to the
WATER HOLE!

COME ON, Timon.

What are you waiting for?

TIMON, stop!

What is it, Pumbaa? You cannot possibly **still** be hungry.

Thirsty?

NOPE.

We are still **LOST**.

I think we should
turn around.

We are not lost.
How many times do
I have to tell you?
The water hole is
THAT WAY!

Help me out here,
will ya?

What do you **MEAN**
we have to turn around?!

FINE.

Have it your way.
Come on, **LET'S GO.**

Lost?! I think I know which way to go, THANK YOU VERY MUCH.

But **FIIIINE.**
You want to go this way?
We'll go this way.

Timon, STOP!

I found a
STREAM!

Maybe we should
follow it.

How many times do
I have to tell you?

I KNOW WHERE I'M GOING!

Sheesh.

You listen to this guy **one time . . .**

What? Fine. Have it your way.
We'll follow the stream.

LOOK.

No **WATER HOLE.**

Just trees and leaves.

What?

You want me to look

THROUGH

the leaves?

SEE?

The water hole!

I **told** you I knew where
I was going.